管弦乐组曲

白求恩在晋察冀

吕其明

Lü Qiming
NORMAN BETHUNE
IN JINGCHAJI DISTRICT
ORCHESTRAL SUITE
SCORE
(1978)

总 谱

上海音乐出版社
SHANGHAI MUSIC PUBLISHING HOUSE

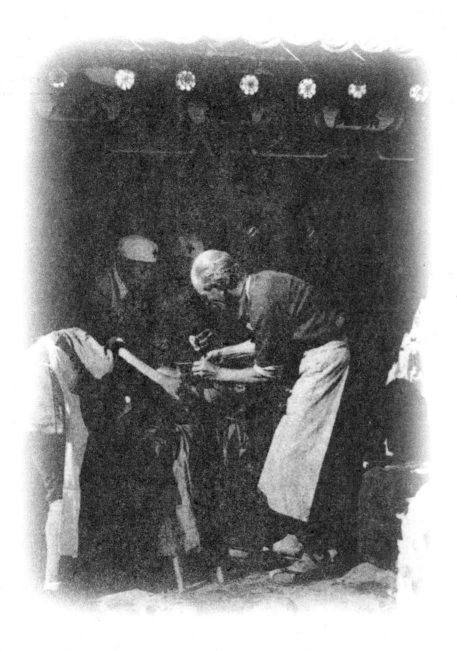

诺尔曼·白求恩（1890-1939），国际主义战士，加拿大共产党员，医生。1936年去西班牙反法西斯前线为西班牙人民服务，1938年率领由加拿大人和美国人组成的医疗队到中国解放区抗日战场工作。他以毫不利己专门利人的精神和高超的医疗技术救治了许多伤员，培养了大批医务干部，为中国人民的解放事业做出了贡献。因医治伤员感染，1939年11月12日逝世于河北唐县。

A brief introduction of Norman Bethune

Norman Bethune (1890-1939), a champion for internationalism, Canadian Communist and doctor. He went to the anti-fascist battlefront in Spain to serve the Spanish in 1936, and worked on the anti-Japanese battlefield in Chinese liberated area in 1938, followed by a medical treatment team that formed by Canadian and American. His altruist and excellent medical-treatment technology saved many wounded people, and trained numbers of doctors and nurses at the same time. He contributed to the liberation of Chinese but died in Tang county of Heber province on November 12th, 1939 because of infection.

我于一九七八年，创作管弦乐组曲《白求恩在晋察冀》，用音乐来讲故事，以表达对白求恩的缅怀、崇敬和赞颂之情，并将这部作品献给伟大的诺尔曼·白求恩。

作者

　　I wrote the orchestral suite "Norman Bethune in Jingchaji District" in 1978, to tell story by music and to place reverence, cherishment on great Norman Bethune.

Composer

乐 队 编 制

Orchestra

曲笛	Qù Dí	Qù Dí
短笛	Flauto Piccolo	Fi.Picc
长笛（2支）	Flautt	Fl
双簧管（2支）（兼英国管）	Oboi(comoingiese)	Ob (cingII)
单簧管（♭B）（2支）	Claneti(♭B)	Cl
大管（2支）	Fagotti	Fag
圆号（F）（4支）	Corni	Cor
小号（♭B）（3支）	Tromboni(♭B)	Trbn
长号（3支）	Tromboni	Trbn
大号	Tuba	Tuba
钟琴	Canpanelli	Campli
竖琴	Arpa	Arpa
定音鼓（4架）	Timpani	Timp
小军鼓	Tambuyo	Tamb
钗（兼吊钗）	Piatti	Piat.
大鼓	Gran Cassa	G.C.
大锣	Tam-Tam	Tam-t.
第一小提琴	Violini	Vl.I
第二小提琴	Violini	Vl.II
中提琴	Viole	Vle
大提琴	Violoncelli	VC.
低音提琴	Contrabassi	Cb

目　　录

第一乐章　不远万里来到中国

Movement I　Made light of traveling thousands of miles to come to China.

站立在白求恩的丰碑和塑像前，肃然起敬，往事钩沉。

Standing before Bethune's monument and statue with reverence, one recalls the past with deep feelings

吕 其 明
Lü Qiming

进入抗日根据地如愿以偿,心潮激荡。

Achieve entering the Anti-Japanese Base Area
with great emotion.

3 **A ppassionato**

第二乐章　马背流动医院
Movement II Flowing hospitals on horses backs.

军号响了,马背流动医院行进在华北平原和崇山峻岭之中。

The bugle is ringing,the flowing hospitals on horse backs march among flat lands in North China and lofty
 mountatins.

第三乐章　战地救护

Movement III　First aid battle field.

伏击战打响了,歼灭日寇！

Ambush operation has fired, annihilating the Japanese invaders！

战场上抢救伤员。

Treating the wounded soldier in battlefield。

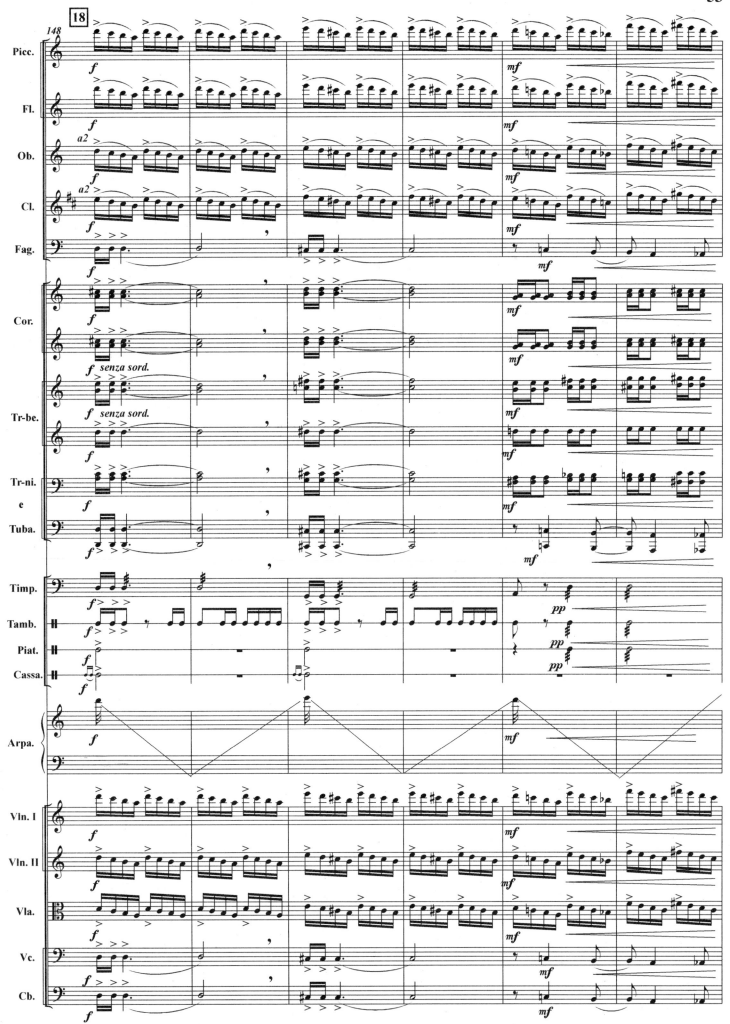

第四乐章　闻笛思乡
Movement IV　Be homesick at the sound of flute.

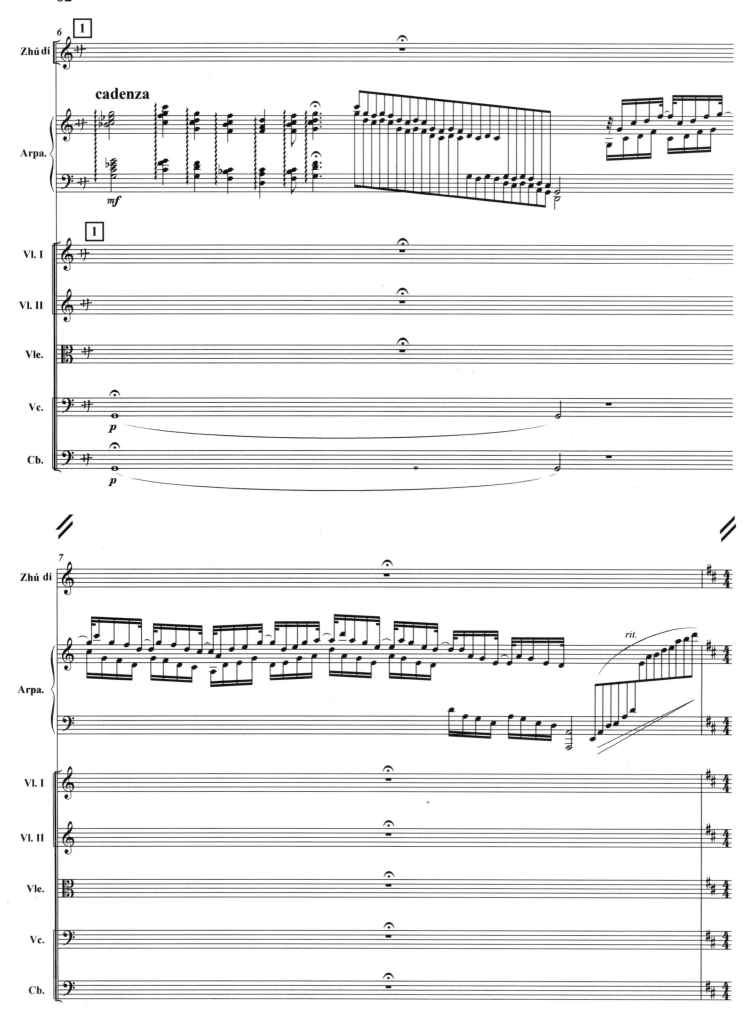

白求恩："这是我的祖国，这是我的人民"。

Bethune:"This is my homeland, they are my people."

不间断连续演奏 *attacca*

第五乐章　永垂不朽
Move ment V　Be immortal.

不幸感染丹毒，根据地军民焦急万分。

He is infected by erysipelas unfortunately, soldiers and people of the basis are all anxious.

巨大的悲痛。
Great distress.

临终遗言。
Last words.

悼念的人越来越多。

More and more people come and mourn.

诺尔曼·白求恩永远活在中国人民心中。

Norman Bethune lives forever in every Chinese people's heart.

14 Brillante Osanna

148
Picc.
Fl.
ppp
cresc.
Ob.
pp
cresc.
Cl.
p cresc.
Fag.
ff
Cor.
pp
p
f
Tr-be.
Tr-ni
e
Tuba.
Timp.
Tamb
Piat.
Gr. C.
vibrafono
cresc.
Arpa.
Vl. I
Vl. II
div.
Vle.
ppp
Vc.
Cb.